"Life and Work" Bible Class
Junior Division

James Henderson
Culcairn
Invergordon

March 1904

ERIC'S GOOD NEWS

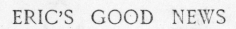

'REX ALWAYS BRINGS ME THINGS FROM THE SEA,' SAID ERIC.

[see p. 19.

Eric's Good News

By Amy Le Feuvre

Author of 'Probable Sons' 'Teddy's Button' 'Odd'
'Dwell Deep' 'On the Edge of a Moor' etc.

'OF SUCH IS THE KINGDOM OF HEAVEN'

SEVENTH EDITION

London
THE RELIGIOUS TRACT SOCIETY
4 Bouverie Street and 65 St. Paul's Churchyard, E.C.

ERIC'S GOOD NEWS

CHAPTER I

SUCH a sweet little face it was, with the curly golden brown hair clustering round the fair white brow, and the deep blue eyes with their gaze of wistful longing. The flush on the soft cheeks betokened delicate health, and many a passer-by noted pityingly the little figure leaning back in the cushioned chair.

But Eric did not heed them; his eyes were fixed on the ocean in front of him, and not even the joyous shouts of the children at play, as they built and demolished their sand castles and forts, seemed to attract him.

His nurse was engrossed in a book ; she was accustomed to her little charge's silent moods, and after settling his cushions and drawing him into the shade of the cliff, now composed herself a little farther off on some flat stones to enjoy an hour's quiet.

' I wonder if it's as tired as I am, poor thing !' came at last from the little lips.

A young man who was lazily reclining some few yards off now looked up sharply as he caught the words.

' I wish it would be tired enough to keep still,' he said.

Eric turned his large blue eyes upon him.

' It tries to be still, but when we are very, *very* tired we can't be.'

'We have not the strength left to

resist the force that drives us; quite true, little chap.'

The child was silent for a minute, then added softly,—

'I saw it asleep yesterday; it was *so* still, just breathing a little, and panting, at the edge. It couldn't help doing that; no one can be quite, quite still.'

The young man smiled, and the two drifted into a quiet, lazy kind of conversation, strange to hear between two such widely opposite characters.

'It's a weary world, isn't it?' asserted the child, with an old-fashioned gravity. 'Nurse is very fond of saying it is, and I think so too.'

'One soon gets to the end of it,' remarked the man with a bitter smile.

'It is all the same, isn't it?—except surprises, and I think I've finished them.'

'How long ago is that, little chap?'

'My last toy from Paris, I think. Father says he won't bring me any more because I didn't feel it a surprise, and I don't care for things if they don't surprise me. I suppose I am too big for surprises now. Everything is always the same, isn't it?'

'Always, little philosopher, when you get accustomed to them.'

'I wondered in one of my thinks to-day if I shall ever see anything very, very wonderful. It seems so long when nothing happens.'

'What would you like to see?'

'Ah, I don't know; I shouldn't like it unless it was a surprise,—something that would make me—make me different. I should like to feel quite, quite comfortable, you know. I mean in my heart. I suppose I mean happy. I should like that wouldn't you?'

'There is none of that kind of happiness in this world, unfortunately.'

'Nurse says there is, but she isn't happy. I think it is only in books and dreams, don't you?'

'It is a fancy, not a fact; but you are rather too small to talk so.'

'I was almost happy once,' and the child's eyes shone with a soft, glad light.

'It was when I was a very little boy, and I went into the country to a farm, and I was very tired, and the woman there caught me up in her arms, and carried me into a long room all red with the fire. It was such a funny room, with plates and dishes all up the walls, and there were baked apples for supper, and pork, and a cat with a bell round its neck, and nurse said I must go to bed, but the woman said "No," and she cuddled me up against her and said: "Bless his darling little heart,

he looks like a motherless bairn as he
is ! "

'She was very fat and soft, you know,
and I sat on her lap all the evening. She
used to tell me such beautiful stories—I
have never heard them since—and father
told me they weren't true ; she said they
were, but I know better now.'

' Puss-in-Boots and Cinderella, eh ?'

'Oh! no, no! Much more lovely.
About a place up there!' and the small
white fingers were raised to the blue sky
above. 'I forget it; a kind of fairyland,
all love and happiness, and something
about a wonderful Man who came down
here from it. She said He loved me, but
I've forgotten now, and father said it wasn't
worth remembering, only made up to
amuse babies!'

There was a curious smile on the young
man's lips. His was a restless, dissatisfied

face, a face on which the traces of a mis-
spent life and of blighted hopes had already
left their marks. Though comparatively
young in years, he was old in the ways of
the world, for he had lived fast ; and because he had exhausted all the resources of
the world's pleasures, and had been dis-
appointed in love, he had now come to the
conclusion that life was not worth living.

He glanced at the innocent young face
beside him, and then up into the un
fathomable blue.

' Not worth remembering !' he muttered,
' why, no—of a certainty not.'

A silence fell on them ; the boy's deep
blue eyes were scanning his fresh acquaintance very closely.

' I like you,' he said quaintly at last,
' because you talk to me as if you understood. Nurse says I'm discontented because I am spoilt, and because I have

everything I want. Father says it is because I am ill, and not like other boys :
but I don't want to be like other boys,
they are so rough and noisy, and they
never do anything but rush about. They
won't sit still and talk to me, and if they
do they say I am " queer," and then they
leave me. Do you think I am queer ? '

' You and I are in the same boat, old
fellow ! We are tired of life, are we not ?
And those who are still enjoying it cannot understand.'

' I want to be happy,' the boy said wistfully, as his eyes wandered over the blue
ocean before him, 'quite happy, right
through, I mean. Do you think I ever
shall be ? '

The young man made no reply, and at
this moment the nurse came towards her
little charge.

' It is time to be going home, Master

Eric,' she said, glancing at his fresh acquaintance as she spoke.

The young man rose to his feet. 'An only child?' he questioned, as he stood in the full strength and power of his manhood looking down at the frail little invalid.

'Yes, sir—only son of Sir Edmund Wallace, who owns most of the property about here.'

Her tone was dignified, and she stooped down to arrange the cushions before she wheeled the little carriage away, adding as she did so :—

'His father has just gone abroad for a month or two, so he feels lonely, poor child !'

But Eric shook his golden head.

'No, I'm not lonely, and I hear very often from father. I like letters, but talking is best. Will you be here to-

morrow, sir? I don't know what your
name is?'

'Captain Graham,' the young man said
with a laugh. 'Yes, perhaps you will find
me here to-morrow.'

They parted, the young captain strolling
away with a cigar in his mouth, and mut-
tering, 'Sir Edmund Wallace, the great
sceptic! Ah, well! I more than half
believe he has right on his side.'

CHAPTER II

ANOTHER morning found this strange couple together, the young man, in spite of his cynical indifference to all around, becoming interested in the quaint, sweet speeches of Eric Wallace.

'There is no one in the world that can manage the sea, is there?' the little fellow said, as he lay watching the rough waves dashing against the breakwater, and scattering themselves in showers of white foam upon all that came in their way.

'No one,' his friend replied. 'Don't you know the story of the king who placed his chair on the sands when the tide was coming in, and forbade the waves to come any farther ? '

' What a silly man !

' He wanted to teach his courtiers a lesson, for they thought him divine.

' What is divine ? '

' Being able to do everything.' The answer was hesitatingly given.

' I should like to be divine. Do you know what I should like to do ? '

' No.'

I should like to be able to sail away up there, to that white cloud, away from everybody and everything, and just lie down and wait till the sun sets, and then sail right into the glory.'

' What glory ? '

' You have seen it—all the golden streaks and pink and red—so lovely— there must be something behind it all. Do you read fairy stories ? '

' I used to, I fancy.'

'Father won't let me read many books ;
he says my brain can't stand it. I am
rather tired of fairies. What kind of books
do you like ? Nurse reads novels, father
reads science. Do you like reading ?'

'I am busy reading the book of Nature
at present, and—you.'

'Now that is nonsense ; you can't read
me !'

A diversion occurred here. Eric's large
retriever, who always accompanied his
little master to the beach, and who had
been gambolling about with other children,
now appeared, after a swim in the sea, with
some tattered leaves in his mouth, which
he dutifully brought to the little invalid's
couch and deposited.

' Good Rex !' said the child, as he took
it from him. 'Rex always brings me
things from the sea, but he knows I don't

like old shoes and rubbish—he used to bring me those, but I taught him not to. This is part of a story-book. Look! I shall dry it and read it, only don't tell nurse; she won't let me read anything now father is away, unless she looks through it first. She says it is as much as her situation is worth!'

The boy was carefully smoothing the wet leaves, and Captain Graham took it from him, saying,—

'It is most likely trash, my boy. I shouldn't keep it.'

But having looked at it, he gave it back to him with a curious smile, saying,—

'That can do you no harm, at all events.'

'Oh, thank you! I like to read when nurse leaves me to get her tea. You see, I get tired of talking to Rex; he is generally with me. Why don't dogs talk, Captain Graham? We do.'

'We are a higher development of human nature,' was the grave reply.

'I don't think dogs get as tired as we do, do they? and they always seem happy. I should not mind being a dog.'

'Without a soul?'

Eric's blue eyes were opened wide.

'What is a soul? Cook says sometimes, "Bless my soul!" and I asked her what it was, and she laughed and said, "A fish." But I didn't believe her, and I asked father, and he said some people thought they had souls, but science proved — I forget now. What do you call a soul?'

'We are getting into deep water; supposing we change the subject. When is your father coming back?'

'Not for a long time. What is a soul, Captain Graham?'

'Upon my word I don't know. It is

supposed to be the quality in us that makes us superior to the animals. Don't you feel yourself much more clever than Rex?'

'No; the only difference is that I can talk and read, and he can't; but then cook's father can't read, and nurse told me she knew some one who couldn't speak. We aren't much alike in looks, are we?'

Captain Graham threw his head back and laughed aloud.

'Not much, my boy, certainly!'

'Do you know I heard nurse's sister say once to her, when they were talking about me and whether I should live to grow up, "Poor little fellow, and his father thinks he will die like a dog!" How does a dog die, Captain Graham?'

'He comes to an end, goes out like a candle: and people say we do not.'

Eric's earnest gaze disconcerted the captain.

'Tell me what you mean. How do we die?'

'What does your father say?'

'He doesn't like me to talk about dying, but he said once it was going to sleep and never waking up. Is that what a dog does?'

'I suppose so.'

Silence fell upon the pair; both were looking out on the ocean, and both were thinking.

At length, a deep sigh from Eric.

'Well, I'm tired enough, anyhow. The time goes *so* slowly, and everything is always the same, it never changes.'

'Life is not attractive to either of us, eh, my boy?'

Eric smoothed out the pages of the

book he held in his hand without re-
plying.

'The —Gospel — according —to — St.
Mark,' he read out slowly ; 'what a funny
name!'

'What is "gospel," Captain Graham?'

'It means "Good News," I believe.

'Do you think this is a true story?'

'I believe so.'

'Have you read it?'

'Yes, I used to read it when I was a
little boy.'

'Is it only a story for little boys?'

'A good many people read it. Look
at the sea this morning, isn't it up-
roarious?'

Eric's blue eyes turned seaward.

'Don't you think it gets angry sometimes? It is quite in a passion this morning,
and no one can manage it. I should like to
see some one who could. It wants to get

beyond the breakwater, and it can't. That's one thing that is able to stop it. It is no good the waves making such a fuss and noise, is it? They never do any good by being so rough.'

'I think they enjoy it. "Come along," say they, "let us upset this boat; it is such fun to see the men floundering about before they sink for ever! And then let us frighten the children and knock down those ridiculous sand forts they're building! If only we could get a little farther and sweep away every creature on the sands, what glorious fun it would be!" Don't you think they would like to have us, Eric?'

'You make them out so cruel. They will be sorry for their roughness soon, and then they'll try and go to sleep—that's when I like them best.'

This proved to be the last of the conversations Eric held with his friend for some days, for Captain Graham went up to London on business, and it was not till a week later that he, sauntering along the sands, cigar in mouth, came upon the invalid carriage with its little occupant.

CHAPTER III

'HULLOO! little chap! you are looking quite spry! What have the doctors been doing to you?'

Eric's weary wistfulness had indeed vanished, and there was a suppressed eagerness and interest in his expressive little face.

He put his little finger to his lips in a quaint, old-fashioned way as he glanced at his nurse, then held out his hand to the captain. Looking up at his strong, stalwart frame, he said very winsomely,—

'Do you like me, Captain Graham?'

'Who does not, you young fisher?'

'But do tell me! are you fond of me?'

Captain Graham laughed heartily as he gazed down at the boy.

'What is coming, Eric? Out with it! Do you know that I have strolled down on purpose to see you this morning? Being one of the most selfish and lazy of human creatures, that says a good deal for your attractive power, let me tell you!'

'I want you,' Eric said softly as he stroked the hand he was still holding, 'I want you to lift me out of the carriage and carry me to that rock over there, and let me sit on your knee, like father does. Only tell nurse you are going to do it first, or she will be coming after us, and I want to have a quite private talk with you!'

It did not take long to carry out this desire, and as Captain Graham held the light little frame in his strong arms, he said,—

'Why, Eric, a puff of wind would blow you away!'

'I am not very heavy, am I? Now then you must listen, please—because my mind seems so very full that I must talk. I have

wanted you *so* much.   You see, I haven't
let nurse see it—she doesn't know I have
it, and you and I understand things together, don't we? You don't call me discontented and peevish, because you feel
like it yourself, don't you? You know
what I mean—you are unhappy and tired
just like me, and we want things to be
new, instead of old.'

'Just so, old philosopher! Go ahead!
I'm listening!'

Eric's eyes grew brighter, and the pink
flush deepened on his cheeks, as he drew
carefully out of his pocket a little brown
paper parcel. Opening it slowly he dis-
closed to Captain Graham's amused gaze
the few pages of the Testament he had
taken home with him.

'You said it was true, Captain Graham,'
the child asserted with an emphatic nod,
and it is wonderful!'

'Is it, my boy? I am glad you have found it so.'

'But, Captain Graham, have you ever read it? Such a story, and such, oh! such a good Man! I love Him! I cried when I was in bed last night because I didn't live when He did! Oh! if I only had! if I only could have just seen Him! and there is such a lot I don't understand, and such a lot I want to ask you about! Do you know, He could do anything? Fancy! He was going to cross the sea one day with some men, and He was so very tired, He just put His head down and went fast to sleep, and the waves got rougher and rougher, and the water came into the boat, and still He was *so* tired He went on sleeping—and then the other men were so frightened that they woke Him up, and told Him He didn't care for them whether they were drowned or not, and then what do you think He

did ? He just stood up and looked, and
saw the rough waves, and all the sea trying
hard to tip the boat over, and He told it
all to be still at once, and it was! Wouldn't
you like to have been there ? And that
isn't all ; He just walked on the top of the
waves another time, when the other men
were all in a boat by themselves, and there
was a storm—He went to them like that !'

The boy's face was enthusiastic as he
looked seaward, and stretching out his
hand, he said as if to the ocean : ' No one
can manage you now, but you have been
made to be still once, and it was grand,
grand ! I should like to have seen you
crushed under His feet ! Oh, Captain
Graham, why did you never tell me about
this wonderful Man before ? '

' Your father is right—you would be a
little enthusiast if —— ' Captain Graham
paused, but Eric looked up earnestly.

'Who is God, Captain Graham?'

'My boy, you are going into matters too deep for you—better give me that book and forget all about it,' and the captain looked uneasy as he ran his fingers through the curly golden hair resting against his shoulder.

'But I *must* know—forget it! as if I could! And it is all true, I feel it is true, and you said it was!'

'Did I? I don't think I did.'

'Captain Graham, isn't it true?'

The startled look in the blue eyes, as they were raised in all trustful innocence to his, stopped the denial already on the young man's lips. As yet, though the little faith he possessed had been nearly extinguished by his wilful acceptance of the doubts that had assailed him, there was in the depths of his heart the remembrance of a mother's faith and teaching, and of

mortal it is! Why, you are quivering from head to foot! Supposing we change the subject. Nothing in this world is worth such excitement.'

'But this is about another world, and that's what I want to know. Is there another world? And how can we get to it? And is Jesus there? Oh! Captain Graham, you might tell me if you know!'

The back of Eric's small hand was brushed hastily across his eyes, but it did not hide the tears already swelling up, and Captain Graham began to realize that the very depths of the child's soul had been stirred, that this was no light matter with him.

'Eric, I will tell you what has been told me, my boy. Now listen!'

Slowly and haltingly, but gathering strength from the intensity of longing and expectation from the blue eyes' upward gaze, Captain Graham told the child the old, old story. First a few words about the creation, then about sin entering the garden, and the plan of salvation, and the future life for each believing soul, Eric now and then stopping him with eager questions, which required clearer explanations.

The time soon slipped away, and Eric's nurse appeared on the scene.

' I am sure it is very kind of the gentleman to be troubled with you, Master Eric. It's rarely, sir, he takes to strangers so. He's such a child for keeping to himself!'

' Captain Graham, will you be here tomorrow?'

' Perhaps I may.'

' My head is so full that I want to have one of my thinks now. But there's a lot more I want to understand.'

' Take care that little head doesn't burst!

I fancy the brains inside are too big for it now.'

And as Captain Graham watched the little carriage being wheeled away, he drew himself up with a stretch and a laugh, saying to himself,—

'I think the world and his wife would be slightly surprised if they had heard me holding forth this morning! It may be worth my while to take up preaching as a vocation—anything for a change!'

CHAPTER IV

IT was a very important little face that looked up into the captain's when next they met.

'I have something to give you, Captain Graham ; I want you to address it for me and send it.'

Is it a letter ?'

'Yes ; you may read it if you like first, in case I may not have written quite properly.' Very carefully and solemnly did Eric take an envelope out of his pocket, and placed it in the captain's hand, and then, with grave scrutiny, his eyes rested on

his friend's face as he turned it over and
then commenced to read it.

If Captain Graham was startled at its
contents he did not show it ; he certainly
tugged the ends of his moustache, and
raised his eyebrows, as he looked at the
name outside it, but as he read on a
softer expression came into his face, and
it was almost reverently that he folded
up the short epistle with its shaky, child-
ish handwriting and replaced it in the
envelope.

This was Eric's letter :—

'To Jesus Christ the Son of God.

'DEAR JESUS,—

'I thought I would like to write to
you to tell you that I love you. I wish I
had known about you before, but I am so
glad you are still alive, and I wish I was
one of those children you took on your

knee, because you were so kind.   I want to ask you something, which is : will you let me come to heaven to see you?   I don't know where it is, but perhaps you can send for me.   I would like to come. My friend Captain Graham says you died to save sinners.   I do not know what a sinner is, but I will ask him more about it.

'I think it was very wicked to kill you, but they could not do it quite ; and I am very glad, and I hope you will answer this letter, and tell me you have got it, and if I can see you soon.

'I am,

'Your loving

'ERIC WALLACE.'

'Will it do, Captain Graham ? You will be able to send it to Him, won't you?'

Eric's tone was anxious.

'No, my boy, I cannot do that. What has become of your wise little head to think of such a thing? How is it to go?'

Eric's lips quivered. 'I thought—I thought the telegraph wires—or balloons—or something—I thought you would know. Oh! Captain Graham, there *must* be a way to heaven! I do want Him to get my letter.'

A quick sob was choked down, and the captain, who had the boy on his knees, drew the curly head and rested it against his shoulder as he said soothingly,—

'Don't cry, Eric; you need never write letters—if you say your prayers it will do just as well.'

'What is prayers?' sobbed out poor Eric.

'Well, talk to Him as you do to me. He hears everything. He is God, you know, and God is a Spirit. He is close to us now, though we cannot see Him, and you have only to speak to Him and He hears at once.'

' Like the fairies?' and Eric raised his wet eyes, hope dawning again in them.

' Fairies! Oh! you believe in them, do you? What a funny little bundle of curiosity you are! Do you believe everything you read?'

' Sometimes I believe in fairies, but not always; and I think they are silly, don't you? But don't talk of fairies. Can Jesus hear what I say whenever I like to talk to Him? Do you mean it really?'

' Yes, I believe He can.'

Eric was silent for a minute, then his eyes fell on the letter.

' And that's no good then,' he said sorrowfully. ' I had better tear it up.'

Captain Graham drew it out of the envelope again and re-read it—half in

amusement, half in pity ; and then sudden-
ly a gust of wind swept past them and
seized the fluttering paper in its clutches,
tossed it wildly in the air, and then carried
it along triumphantly, until it was lost to
sight round the corner of the cliff.

Eric watched it with parted lips and
flushed cheeks ; then, in a solemn whisper,
he asserted,—

'God has told the wind to blow it up to
Him ; so He does want to see it, doesn't
He ?'

'It looks like it, certainly,' was the
reply.

'I'm so glad, it took me so long to write;
and now, Captain Graham, what is a sinner ?'

'Anybody who sins—does bad things—
is wicked.   Anything wrong is a sin.'

'Nurse says telling lies and hiding
things is wrong.   I expect I'm a sinner—

I have been hiding this story of Jesus from nurse ; is that wrong ?'

' I expect so.'

'Are you a sinner ? I mean, have you ever been one when you were a little boy like me ?'

'We are all sinners, Eric. The bigger the man the bigger the sinner, I believe. Yes, I am a pretty big sinner, I expect.'

' I'm so glad,' said Eric cheerfully; 'then Jesus died for you and me. I don't quite know what that means ; but it's something good, didn't you say ? Tell me again why He died.'

' Upon my word, Eric, I can't explain it. Your book tells you.'

It's rather difficult to understand, Captain Graham, and you did tell me about it yesterday. Tell me again.'

' Well, I believe if He had not died we

couldn't have gone to heaven, and now we can.'

'When can we?'

'When we die.'

'But I have heard they put people in the ground. How can they go to heaven?'

'That is only their bodies. We are supposed to have souls that leave our bodies, and that part of us goes to heaven.'

'It's *beautiful*!' exclaimed Eric with shining eyes; 'and now tell me what heaven is like?'

'I don't know'—a gleam of humour shot into the captain's eye—'I have never been there, you see.'

'But you told me yesterday a lot about it.'

'Oh, that was what the Bible tells us about it.'

'The Bible? That is what father told me wasn't fit for little boys. Go on—tell me about heaven.'

'It is a kind of fairyland, Eric : all goodness and happiness, and everybody and
everything quite perfect. No worries, no
bills or duns for money, no deceivers, nothing hollow or sham, no hypocrisies and pre-
tences, nothing to mar one's enjoyment.'

'And—Jesus there !' broke in the child's
voice softly ; 'that will be best of all. If
He would take me up in His arms I
should be quite, quite happy for ever. Do
you think He would ?'

'I think He might.'

'But why couldn't we have gone to
heaven without Jesus dying ? That's what
I don't understand.'

'Because God could not let a sinner enter
heaven. He said we must be punished for
sin, and that was separation from Him for
ever ; and then Jesus Christ said, as He
was not a sinner, He could be punished instead of us ; so He came down from hea-

ven and lived a good life here, to show us
how we ought to live. When He died it
is supposed that He bore all our sins on
Him then, and so God forgave us.'

'And now you and I are going to
heaven?'

'I don't know about that.'

'But you said we were sinners. We are,
aren't we?'

'A good many sinners will be shut out
of heaven, Eric—so people say.'

'Why?'

'I am a bad hand at this, my boy.
Don't you think we have had enough of
it?'

'But,' objected Eric, his lower lip droop-
ing pitifully, 'I don't want to be shut out
of heaven, Captain Graham, and I don't
understand you. You change round. You
said Jesus died to let us go to heaven—
why can't we go?'

'So you can—and you are pretty sure to get there, too!'

'Then you can, too, can't you?'

'If I wanted too, I suppose I could.'

'But don't you want to?'

'I have not thought about it.'

Eric looked puzzled, but he had faith in his captain, and felt sure if his words at times were difficult to understand, it was because he was grown up, and knew a great deal more than himself.

'My doctor is coming to see me to-morrow,' he said, after a long pause; 'he comes from London every two or three months to see me; so I shan't be here to-morrow morning. He is very kind, but he does poke me about so, and always goes away saying, "You must rouse yourself, my boy!" As if he hadn't roused me enough by all his pokes and shakings!'

'What does he think he can do for you?'

'He told father once there was no reason why I shouldn't live to be a strong man.　He said I wanted to be roused and amused, and then father took me round the world in his yacht, but I was no better after and I got tired of that before I had got half round!'

'You are hard to please, youngster!'

'Not now I shouldn't be, Captain Graham, that tired feeling has nearly gone; only I wish I understood more about the things in my Good News.'

A still longer interval now elapsed before Eric met his friend again.　The weather proved stormy, and the beach was deserted by all save those who considered themselves impervious to wind and rain.

Captain Graham grew restless as he paced up and down in his comfortable quarters at the Royal Hotel.

'I have stayed here long enough,

Thank goodness my leave is nearly out! Any kind of work will be better than this; and yet how sick I am of our set of fellows! I have half a mind to sell out, but what on earth should I do with myself then! I cannot imagine what is keeping me here, unless it is that child. He ought to be put in a book. The correct thing is for him to die, I suppose, but he seems to have taken a new lease of life. I can fancy his father's wrath when he comes home and discovers what subject is engrossing his thoughts. Shall I be held up as his teacher, I wonder?'

And this thought was so ludicrous that Captain Graham indulged in a hearty laugh; yet there was a hollowness in his mirth, and a heavy sigh quickly followed.

CHAPTER V

'BROUGHTON MANOR.'

'MY DEAR FRIEND,—

'I want you to come and see me. Nurse said you would not be troubled, but I know you will. I can't go out because it is raining so. I am very happy, and I have written to father and told him all about it. Nurse has been very angry, but she says she's only angry because father will be angry. I don't know what she means, and I want you to tell me. Come soon, please. Doctor Parker has told me a lot more.

'Your dear friend

'ERIC WALLACE.

This was the note handed to Captain Graham as he was at luncheon a day or two afterwards, and an hour after found the captain swinging along in his mackintosh towards Broughton Manor, a large bag of hot-house grapes protruding from one pocket, and a packet of French bon-bons in the other.

He found Eric on a couch in a luxuriously furnished room, overlooking the fine old park that surrounded the manor.

His face lighted up as he held out his little hand to his visitor.

'I knew you would come. I have missed you so! I have such a lot to tell you! There is father's easy chair there —it's a very comfortable one, and I don't mind your sitting in it, though I never let any one else, not even my doctor.'

Captain Graham seated himself with a

E

smile, then brought out his gifts, and Eric's
face brightened again.

'You are a kind friend,' he said quaintly,
as he held out both hands for the parcels.
'Do you know, you are the first visitor I've
had here—all for myself!—and we will just
be like two gentlemen together.   First we
will have a talk, and then we will have the
wine in—like father does—or do you like
whiskey? and I have asked Simmonds—
that's our old butler—to go and buy some
very best cigars and bring in on a tray for
you.   I dare say you won't mind smoking
alone—I shan't smoke till I'm a man, but
I shall like to see you—just like father's
friends—they always like a good cigar
before they go.'

'Thank you,' said Captain Graham
gravely, though his eyes twinkled in spite
of himself, 'that will be very pleasant.
Now, what have you been doing with

yourself during this stormy weather? Been moped to death, eh?'

'Oh no, no! Why, Captain Graham, here Eric leant forward impressively, his blue eyes glistening with emotion, 'I have been learning to know Jesus. Would you like to hear?'

Captain Graham leant back in his chair and crossed his legs.

'Very much, Eric,' was his answer.

'Well, it was my doctor who helped me. When he came to poke me about, I said to him, " Isn't it a pity, doctor, that Jesus isn't here to make me well without any poking? I wonder if you know about Him?" And then he said he did, and he sat down and told me a lot—just the same as you did; and he told me just to speak to Him as if He were standing by my chair, because He was really there, only I couldn't see Him. And then he knelt down on the carpet

just here, between you and me, and he
spoke to Him himself ; and then he asked
me if I would like to speak to Him, so
after a few minutes I did. I felt rather
shy, you know, at first.'

' And what did you say, my boy ? '

' I said : " My dear Jesus, I hope you'll
excuse me speaking to you, because I know
you're a wonderful person, but my Good
News tells me you're so kind to children
that I know you'll listen to me. I want to
thank you so much for dying for me, and I
am glad to find out that I am a sinner,
because you are fond of sinners. I don't
know you very well yet, but I do love you.
Will you please be my friend, and will you
talk to me when I'm feeling uncomfortable
and lonely ? " I think that was all I said to
Him—I remembered Him that I had sent
Him a letter, and asked Him if He liked it.
I think that was all.'

'And what happened then?'

'Well, then my doctor told me a lot more. Fancy! I can ask the Lord Jesus for anything I want, and if it is good for me He will give it to me! I suppose you know that, don't you, Captain Graham?'

'Yes, I suppose I do.'

'But isn't it lovely? And I've asked Him such heaps and heaps of things! And He has answered some already. I asked Him to give Sarah's mother some washing—Sarah is one of the housemaids who's very good to me, and her mother is so badly off she can't get meat more than on Sundays—and He sent her a lady yesterday who gave her some—Sarah told me this morning; and I've asked Him to find our black kitten and send her home, and not to let father be angry, as nurse says he will be; and I asked Him to make you come and see me to-day,

—nurse said you would not be bothered,—
and then I told Him about cook, who will
send me up rice puddings for dinner, and
says they're good for little boys, when she
knows I don't like them.   I asked Jesus to
make the rice bad, so that she couldn't cook
it; and then I remembered Simmonds'
nephew, who has broken his leg and has
had to leave off being a sailor, and his
young lady, Simmonds' says, won't look at
him, so I've asked Him to make her kinder.
I can't tell you all.   I talk and I talk to
Him, and the best of all is, that He is
never tired of listening, my doctor says,
and then He is always with me.'

   ' And how did your doctor find you, Eric,
—better ? '

   ' Yes, much better.   He says I have
found the medicine that would make me
well at last.   I don't know quite what he
meant, do you ? '

' I think he may have meant you had found something to interest you, my boy.'

' Well, I don't feel tired inside now. This is the very biggest surprise I have ever had. I wish some one had told me about it before. And then, Captain Graham, I find that I can do things that please Jesus. He likes me to be patient, and not tell nurse she is a cross-patch, and not throw my medicines away when they are nasty. He wants me to grow up as much like Him as I can be ; and of course you know this gives me a lot to do, because I have to stop and think very often before I do things. I used to try to be good because nurse said I ought, but I know now it makes Him sorry and grieved, and I don't want to make Him sorry, I *do* love Him so ! '

Eric leant back on his cushions with a sigh of happiness as he paused for breath, whilst Captain Graham gazed thoughtfully out of the window.

'It seems to me, Eric, that you have learnt all you can learn, and more than most in this world. I have something else in my pocket for you. I am leaving in a week's time; I have to go back to my regiment; so I thought I would give you a complete copy of your Good News, as you call it. If your father doesn't like it he must take it from you when he comes back. You have got something in your head now that he will not be able to take away very easily, and if it makes your life happier it would be cruelty to deprive you of it. Tell your nurse that I gave it to you, and that, as things are, she had best let you have it.'

Captain Graham placed a New Testament in the little fellow's hand. It was a handsome copy, bound in Russian leather, an when Eric knew what it was his face grew perfectly radiant.

'You're *very* good to me; I don't know what I shall do when you're gone. I wish you wouldn't go. You see, you know all about these things, and we can talk about them together; I shall have nobody if you go. My doctor isn't coming down to see me for a long time. Would you be very angry if I just ask the Lord Jesus to make you stay?'

'I think you had better not, Eric. Look! I do think the weather is breaking! There is the sun again. Won't you be glad to be down on the beach to-morrow if it is fine?'

'Yes,' said Eric contentedly, as he fingered his new treasure, 'and I hope you will meet me there; will you?'

'Very likely; but I think I must be going now.'

'Wait a moment. Will you ring that bell, please ? I can't get up.'

And then when a solemn old butler appeared, bearing wine and cigars, Eric, with all the gravity of an old man, offered them to his friend, and Captain Graham accepted them with equal gravity, though he found that a difficult task, when Eric, with a wave of his little hand towards him, addressed the butler as follows :—

'This is my friend, Simmonds. You haven't seen him before. He is a very old friend now, and a very nice one. I like him better than the friends you and nurse try to find for me ; but then I chose him myself—at least, we did it together ; didn't we, Captain Graham ?'

'That we certainly did, Eric.'

'And, Simmonds, Captain Graham has brought me the most beautiful Good News that you ever saw, with a lot more

in it than mine has ; and it's Captain Graham, you know, that has made me happy at
last, so you ought to thank him. You
were always saying you wished I wouldn't
be so miserable. He told me all about
Jesus first.'

The old butler smiled benignantly on the
child.

'He does look wonderful better, sir,
excuse me,' and then noiselessly he slipped
out of the room ; and after a few minutes
Captain Graham took his leave.

As he tramped back to the town his
thoughts were busy.

'It is a wonderful thing for satisfying a
child's soul,' he said to himself. 'I wonder
if it will last, and if by any possibility—
granted that I could believe in it—whether
it would satisfy mine !'

CHAPTER VI

THE weather broke, and there were very few mornings that did not find the young soldier on the beach by the side of his little friend. Sometimes Eric would ask to have a chapter read out of his Testament, and then would follow an earnest discussion ; at least, if the earnestness was only on the child's side, Captain Graham did not let him see it, and the questions and deductions that sprang up struck the captain as startlingly fresh and conclusive.

But the last morning came, and Eric's bright little face grew very sad when the time of parting drew near.

'Will you write to me sometimes, Captain Graham? I shall be thinking of you so often.'

'I promise to send you a line now and then, my boy.'

'And, Captain Graham, I've been very puzzled lately—I can't make it out—and I'm so sorry.'

Here Eric paused, gazed wistfully up at the face of his friend, and then shook his head very sorrowfully.

'What is up now?' enquired Captain Graham in an amused tone.

Eric slipped his little hand into the strong one that was laid on his shoulder.

I wonder why you are so unhappy, if you have known all about Jesus. I should never have been if I had known before. and yet you were just as tired and unhappy as I was.

'It isn't so fresh to me as it is to you, Eric.'

The captain's tone was hesitating; he could not bear that the boy's faith in himself should be shaken, and yet truth compelled him to undeceive him.

'I had forgotten all about these things, my boy. They don't touch me as they do you. It is my own fault, I suppose. You know much more about them already than I ever did.'

'Why,' said Eric, with open eyes, 'you have told me all yourself! And you have explained all the hard things so beautifully. Why, Captain Graham, if it hadn't been for you I should never have known about Jesus.'

'It isn't the knowing about Him, Eric; all we professing Christians have the head knowledge, but the majority in our country are not much the better for it. Don't

puzzle your little head over me. You are
a happy little soul in your belief, keep so,
and when you pray to your new Friend
don't forget me.'

Eric nodded brightly. 'He knows all
about you, Captain Graham, I have told
Him everything. I will ask Him to make
you happier. He is *sure* to do it. Oh!
must you go? Oh! Captain Graham!'

And though it was on the beach the
young soldier was not ashamed to stoop
down and have two little clinging arms
round his neck, and two little quivering lips
pressed tightly against his bronzed cheek.

'Good-bye. I'll try not to miss you.
I don't mind disappointments so much
now, but I shan't never, *never*, forget
you!'

Poor little Eric's ungrammatical sentence
rang in the captain's ears as he walked
away : ' I shan't never, never, forget you,'

and he grimly wondered what his brother officers would say if they knew in whose society the latter part of his leave had been spent.

'Ah! well!' he muttered, 'I envy that child's faith and happiness, and more than half feel inclined to follow his example. It is not a religion he has got hold of, but a real Person—it makes a vast difference, I fancy!'

Captain Graham rejoined his regiment, and his life went on in the old way. Yet ne looked forward with a strange pleasure to the letters that arrived from Eric, and vainly endeavoured to stifle the uneasy, restless longings in his own heart. It was after receiving one of these quaint epistles one evening that the young man retired to his room with a fixed purpose in his mind— that of settling, once for all, whether there was anything in this religion for him, or whether it was only suitable for innocent children and weak, credulous women.

'I cannot stand the worry of it much longer,' was his angry thought. 'I cannot imagine why it has taken such a hold on me—do what I will, I can get no rest from it, night or day!'

And then again he spread the child's letter before him.

'MY DEAR, DEAR FRIEND,——

'I was so happy to get your nice letter, and I like hearing about the bugles and the soldiers and your clever horse. I'm getting well so fast that my doctor wrote and said perhaps I could ride on a pony soon, instead of being drawn in my carriage. I should like that. My dear father is very ill. He has never written to me since I wrote to him and told him what a Good News I had found. He wrote to nurse and told her not

F

'Except ye be converted, and become
as little children, ye shall not enter into the
kingdom of heaven.'

'Whosoever therefore shall humble himself as this little child, the same is greatest
in the kingdom of heaven.'

Long did he ponder. When midnight

came it found Captain Graham on his knees.

'Lord, I believe; help Thou my unbelief!

CHAPTER VII

My dear Friend,—

'I am in trouble, and I have been crying all day : my dear, dear father is dead, and I shall not see him till I go to heaven. Nurse heard it yesterday, and my doctor came to see me to-day, and my aunt, who I don't know at all, because she said my father asked her not to see me, only she was with him when he died, because he was coming back, and he did not die till he landed at Plymouth. My aunt knows all about Jesus, and she loves Him like you and I do, and I am so glad you are quite happy

now. My aunt gave me a part of dear
father's letter that he had begun to write to
me, but he could not finish it. And he told
her to take me to live with her, or else she
was to come and live with me, so she has
come here because I don't want to go away.
My aunt says I can send you father's letter.
I told her next to father I loved you, and
she said you would like to see it, and she
told me you would understand father's
letter best if you saw mine that I wrote to
him, which he kept under his pillow and
gave to my aunt when she came away from
him. I don't quite understand, but I send
them both, and will you come and see me?
I am really quite unhappy to have dear
father die, but I have told the Lord Jesus,
and I sit quiet and He comforts me.

'Your loving friend

'Eric.'

This was Eric's letter to his father :—

' MY DARLING FATHER,—

' I have a lot to tell you to-day, and you will be so glad to know I am happy at last. I have found the wonderfullest book, which means Good News, and it is all true. It came from the sea, and Rex brought it in his mouth, and Captain Graham told me a lot more. I wish I could tell you what's in it, but I can't write so much. There's a wonderful Man, so good and kind, in it. I loved Him when I read about Him, and He really was alive once, only He was killed, but He came alive again because no one had any business to kill Him. He was GOD, and He went up to heaven in the sky, but He has not only stayed there, He goes all about the world still, only we can't see Him, and He loves everybody, and He loves me and He loves you. His name is

the Lord Jesus ; have you heard of Him,
dear father ? because you never told me.
My captain told me all about it : how He
died because He wanted us to go to a
beautiful place in the sky, and we could not
have gone there if He hadn't ; He didn't
mind how much He was hurt as long as
He could make us happy by being hurt
Himself; and He likes us to speak to Him,
and He always hears, and Doctor Parker
says He will give me anything I ask for
if it's good for me.   My Good News says
He likes sinners, and I have found that
I am a sinner, and so is my captain.   Are
you a sinner, dear father ?   I hope you
are, because Jesus died for sinners.   It
is so lovely to have Jesus to talk to now.
I tell Him all, and I never feel lonely no
more, and He loves me, I feel He does.
Nurse says you will be angry ; you won't
be, will you ? She never tells me why. Her

niece's daughter has got a husband. He is
our keeper's son. Simmonds says she's a
wonderful smart girl. Rex killed a little
chicken yesterday. Bob beat him, and he
came crying to me. Is a dog a sinner, dear
father? I hope you will write me a nice
long letter and come back soon.

' Your own loving son

' ERIC.'

The father's letter was this :—

MY DEAREST LITTLE SON,—

' I have been waiting to write to you a
long time, and I have torn up three letters,
and your aunt has refused to send another,
so I must begin again. Your poor old father
is very ill, Eric, and I am afraid you will
never see him again. I received your last
letter, and have read it many, many times.
I am so glad to hear from Dr. Parker that
my boy is in better health and spirits. I

hope you will grow up a strong man yet, able to manage your life better than your father has done, for, Eric, I feel I have made a mess of mine. One does not realize it till one is brought upon a dying bed.

'Yes—believe in what and in whom you please, Eric; may it make you happier than my creeds have made me! I never talked to you about the things that are filling your little head at present simply because— there! I will write no more. Think gently of me, and when you pray remember me in your prayers. One thing I lay upon you as a command : burn every single book in my library and every MS. you find, all my letters, all my notes—spare none.

'Good-bye, my little son. Your aunt—'
(' N.B. Your father is too weak to finish this, Eric. I —your aunt—will come and tell you all.

'FLORENCE WALLACE.')

Captain Graham read these letters in his room.

'Poor little chap! I wonder if his father found the light at last! Ah! Eric, if that were so, you will have brought two wanderers into the kingdom of heaven.'

FINIS.

London : Printed by William Clowes & Sons, Ltd., Duke Street, Stamford Street, S.E., and 28, Great Windmill Street, W.

Some Popular Stories

ILLUSTRATED
by the
BEST ARTISTS
of the
PRESENT AGE

Published by

The Religious Tract Society

4 Bouverie St. & 65 St. Paul's Churchyard

POPULAR BOYS' TALES.

By TALBOT BAINES REED.

THE ADVENTURES OF A THREE-GUINEA WATCH.
Illustrated. Large crown 8vo, 3s. 6d.

THE COCK HOUSE AT FELLSGARTH.
A Public School Story. Illustrated. Large crown 8vo, 3s. 6d.

A DOG WITH A BAD NAME.
Illustrated. Large crown 8vo, 3s. 6d.

THE FIFTH FORM AT ST. DOMINIC'S.
A School Story. Illustrated. Large crown, 8vo, 3s. 6d.

THE MASTER OF THE SHELL.
Illustrated. Large crown 8vo, 3s. 6d.

MY FRIEND SMITH.
Illustrated. Large crown 8vo, 3s. 6d.

PARKHURST SKETCHES, AND OTHER STORIES.
Illustrated. Crown 8vo, 2s. 6d.

REGINALD CRUDEN.
A Tale of City Life. Illustrated. Large crown 8vo, 3s. 6d.

TOM, DICK, AND HARRY.
Illustrated. Large crown 8vo, 3s. 6d.

LONDON:
THE RELIGIOUS TRACT SOCIETY,
4 BOUVERIE ST. AND 65 ST. PAUL'S CHURCHYARD.

The 'Brave Deeds' Series.

A SERIES OF CHEAP GIFT BOOKS.

Large crown 8vo, cloth gilt, **2s.** each.

BRAVE DEEDS OF YOUTHFUL HEROES.
True Stories from Life. Profusely Illustrated. Cloth gilt, 2s.

'Excellent illustrations and well-written adventures from a wide field.'—*Guardian*.

THE ROMANCE OF REAL LIFE.
True Incidents in the Lives of the Great and Good. Freely Illustrated. Cloth gilt, 2s.

'"The Romance of Real Life" should be put into the hands of young people. It is written down to them, and shows once again that truth is stranger than fiction. The book is well illustrated—and, what is a great consideration in looking for prizes, there is plenty of it for the money.'—*Methodist Times*.

'A handsome volume. Boys and girls will assuredly derive pleasure from the perusal of this book.'—*Daily Chronicle*.

STRANGE TALES OF PERIL AND ADVENTURE.
With Twenty-three Illustrations. Cloth gilt, 2s.

ADVENTURES ASHORE AND AFLOAT.
With Fifteen Illustrations. Cloth gilt, 2s.

THE CRUISE OF THE 'MARY ROSE.'
By W. H. G. KINGSTON, Author of 'Captain Cook,' 'Ben Hadden,' 'The Golden Grasshopper,' etc. With Fifteen Illustrations. Cloth gilt, 2s.

WIND AND WAVE.
A Story of the Siege of Leyden, 1574. By H. E. BURCH, Author of 'Dick Delver,' 'More than Conqueror,' etc. With Fifteen Illustrations. Cloth gilt, 2s.

LONDON:

THE RELIGIOUS TRACT SOCIETY,
4 BOUVERIE ST. AND 65 ST. PAUL'S CHURCHYARD.

G

THE 'BRAVE DEEDS' SERIES—*Continued.*

CEDAR CREEK.

From the Shanty to the Settlement. A Tale of Canadian Life. By the Author of 'The Foster Brothers of Doon,' etc. With Fifteen Illustrations. Cloth gilt, 2s.

ONCE UPON A TIME;

Or, The Boy's Book of Adventures. With Fifteen Illustrations. Cloth gilt, 2s.

'Very good the stories are. They take us to the South Seas and the Alps, to Oregon, Northumberland, and the Hooghley, and we are incidentally introduced to wreckers, beachcombers, brigands, cannibals, and herring-fishers.'—*Times.*

THE BLACK TROOPERS.

And other Stories. With Fifteen Illustrations. Cloth gilt, 2s.

A RACE FOR LIFE.

And other Tales. With Fifteen Illustrations. Cloth gilt, 2s.

A BOOK OF HEROES.

By HENRY JOHNSON, Author of 'Untrue to his Trust,' etc. With Fifteen Illustrations. Cloth gilt, 2s.

'There is not one of the stories but well deserves the place assigned to it in the instructive and inspiring volume which it helps to make up.'—*Glasgow Herald.*

"Mr. Henry Johnson has avoided the conventional method of telling these stories of doughty deeds and brave endurance.'—*Sheffield Independent.*

NOBLE DEEDS OF THE WORLD'S HEROINES.

By HENRY CHARLES MOORE. With Fifteen Illustrations. Cloth gilt, 2s.

This is a record of deeds of daring and heroism performed by women — women who 'counted not their lives dear unto them' so long as duty called for the sacrifice.

The intrepid deeds of some twenty-nine women are recounted, among whom may be mentioned Alice Ayres and the Union Street Fire, Mary Rogers the Stewardess of the *Stella*, and Olivia Ogren and her marvellous escape from the Boxers.

LONDON:

THE RELIGIOUS TRACT SOCIETY,

4 BOUVERIE ST. AND 65 ST. PAUL'S CHURCHYARD.

THE RELIGIOUS TRACT SOCIETY'S
'ENLARGED' SHILLING SERIES.

Each Volume contains not less than 160 pages.
With Illustrations. Crown 8vo, **1s.**

THE 'ENLARGED' SHILLING SERIES
—*Continued.*

THE 'ENLARGED' SHILLING SERIES
—Continued.

23. **Palissy, the Huguenot Potter.**
    By C. L. BRIGHTWELL, Author of 'The Romance of Modern Missions,' etc.

24. **It's All Real True.**
    By EGLANTON THORNE, Author of 'A Little Protestant in Rome,' etc.

25. **Paul Harvard's Campaign.**
    By EVELYN EVERETT-GREEN, Author of 'Dick Whistler's Tramp,' etc.

26. **Dorothy Tresilis; or, Down at Polwin.**
    By M. M. POLLARD, Author of 'Cora,' 'Only Me,' etc.

27. **Dolly.**
    By M. F. WILSON.

28. **Dora.**
    A Tale of Influence.

29. **Gipsy Jan.**
    By NELLIE HELLIS, Author of 'Higher Up,' etc.

30. **Led into Light.**
    By LUCY TAYLOR, Author of 'The Wishing Well,' etc.

31. **Sailor Jack.**
    A Tale of the Southern Seas. By CONSTANCE CROSS.

32. **Honour, not Honours.**
    By Mrs. AUSTIN DOBSON, Author of 'Cherryburn,' etc.

33. **Morva Hall.**
    By JENKIN JONES, Author of 'Ivor Rees,' 'Shad's Cottage,' etc.

34. **Fritz of the Tower.**
    A Tale of the Franco-German War. By L. LOBENHOFFER.

35. **The Brydges.**
    A Story of Three Homes. By the Author of 'Margie's Gifts,' etc.

LONDON:
THE RELIGIOUS TRACT SOCIETY,
4 BOUVERIE ST. AND 65 ST. PAUL'S CHURCHYARD.

The 'Snowdrop' Series.

Each containing 192 pages and upwards. With Illustrations
Crown 8vo, cloth gilt, 1s. 6d.

1. CITY SPARROWS, AND WHO FED THEM.

By RUTH LYNN. With Three Illustrations by ALFRED
PEARSE.

2. THE SECRET ROOM.

A Story of Tudor Times. By L. POCKLINGTON. With
Three Illustrations by RAYMOND POTTER.

3. THE GREAT SALTERNS.

By SARAH DOUDNEY, Author of 'Lady Dye', Reparation,' 'Janet Darney's Story,' etc.

4. HAROLD'S FRIENDS;

Or, The New Rector of Greythorpe. By C. A.
BURNABY, Author of 'Our Story,' 'Tom Larkins,'
'Fred Ferns's Decision,' etc.

5. THE TWINS THAT DID NOT PAIR.

By H. LOUISA BEDFORD, Author of 'Daniel's Fallen
Dagon,' 'I will be a Sailor,' 'A Maid whom there were
None to Praise,' etc.

LONDON:
THE RELIGIOUS TRACT SOCIETY,
4 BOUVERIE ST. AND 65 ST. PAUL'S CHURCHYARD.

STORIES FOR GIRLS

By MRS. GEORGE DE HORNE VAIZEY

(JESSIE MANSERGH).

ABOUT PEGGY SAVILLE.

Illustrated. Crown 8vo, cloth gilt, 2s. 6d.

'Somewhat in the vein of Miss Charlotte Yonge is "Peggy Saville." A brightly told and sensible story concerning a group of youths and maidens who filled their home with glee, tempered by the anxiety of their elders.'— *Pall Mall Gazette.*

'A charming girl's story. Peggy is a singularly attractive personage, and around her the whole interest of the tale revolves.'— *Westminster Gazette.*

MORE ABOUT PEGGY.

Illustrated. Crown 8vo, cloth gilt, 2s. 6d.

'Peggy is of all young women the most delightful—vivacious, bold, timid, and tender by turns.'— *Literature.*

'The story is invigorating, its incidents vivid, and altogether the book possesses a delightful charm which will secure its success.'— *Methodist Times.*

'Peggy is delicious. Those who traced her earlier adventures will be delighted to renew acquaintance with her.'— *Baptist Times.*

A HOUSEFUL OF GIRLS.

Illustrated. Crown 8vo, cloth gilt, 2s. 6d.

'No girl can fail to be fascinated by the six bonny, healthy, fun-loving, and keen-hearted English lasses who constitute the household. The various characters are thoroughly well drawn. Moreover, these "lassies" are modern, and ride their bicycles, learn wood-carving and cooking, and make their own blouses.'— *Methodist Times.*

'Six fair maidens, a bevy of bright, intelligent lasses with a dear, wise, little mother, appear before us in various scenes of domestic life. The amusing chatter of their gay and merry tongues, their innocent escapades, the clouds that occasionally gather over their home, their philanthropic enterprises, and their love affairs, fill the book with passages that entice the reader to the end.'— *Baptist.*

'One would be puzzled to name a more facile, fascinating, and daintily humorous writer about girls than the creator of "Peggy Saville."'— *Bookseller.*

LONDON:

THE RELIGIOUS TRACT SOCIETY,

4 BOUVERIE ST. AND 65 ST. PAUL'S CHURCHYARD.

STORIES

By EVELYN EVERETT-GREEN.

BARBARA'S BROTHERS.

With Frontispiece. Crown 8vo, 2s. 6d.

THE HEAD OF THE HOUSE.

With Frontispiece. Crown 8vo, 2s. 6d.

JOINT GUARDIANS.

With Frontispiece. Crown 8vo, 2s. 6d.

LENORE ANNANDALE'S STORY.

Illustrated. Crown 8vo, 2s. 6d.

THE MISTRESS OF LYDGATE PRIORY.

With Frontispiece. Crown 8vo, 2s. 6d.

OLD MISS AUDREY.

With Frontispiece. Crown 8vo, 2s. 6d.

TWO ENTHUSIASTS.

With Frontispiece. Crown 8vo, 2s. 6d.

THE PERCIVALS;

Or, A Houseful of Girls. With Frontispiece. Crown 8vo, 2s. 6d.

SIR REGINALD'S WARD;

Or, Tales of the Family. Illustrated. Crown 8vo, 2s. 6d.

TOM HERON OF SAX.

With Frontispiece. Crown 8vo, 2s. 6d.

UNCLE ROGER;

Or, a Summer of Surprises. Illustrated. Imperial 16mo, 2s. 6d.

LONDON:

THE RELIGIOUS TRACT SOCIETY,

4 BOUVERIE ST. AND 65 ST. PAUL'S CHURCHYARD.

STORIES

By EVELYN EVERETT-GREEN.

THE FAMILY.

Some Reminiscences of a Housekeeper. Illustrated. Large crown 8vo, 5s.

ALWYN RAVENDALE.

With Frontispiece by HAROLD COPPING. Large crown 8vo, 3s. 6d.

FIR-TREE FARM.

Illustrated. Large crown 8vo, 3s. 6d.

THE CONSCIENCE OF ROGER TREHERN.

With Frontispiece by HAROLD COPPING. Large crown 8vo, 3s. 6d.

THE SUNNY SIDE OF THE STREET.

A Story of Patient Waiting. Illustrated. Crown 8vo, 2s.

TREGG'S TRIUMPH.

A Story of Stormy Days. Illustrated. Crown 8vo, 2s.

DICK WHISTLER'S TRAMP.

Illustrated. Crown 8vo, 1s.

PAUL HARVARD'S CAMPAIGN.

Illustrated. Crown 8vo, 1s.

LONDON:

THE RELIGIOUS TRACT SOCIETY,

4 BOUVERIE ST. AND 65 ST. PAUL'S CHURCHYARD.

BOOKS–CHIEFLY FOR GIRLS.

BY RUTH LAMB.

HOLIDAY STORIES.
Illustrated. Crown 8vo, 3s. 6d.

ARTHUR GLYN'S CHRISTMAS-BOX.
Illustrated. Crown 8vo, 2s. 6d.

HER OWN CHOICE.
Illustrated. Crown 8vo, 2s. 6d.

IN THE TWILIGHT SIDE BY SIDE.
Crown 8vo, 2s. 6d. ; Paper Covers, 1s. 6d.

MORE TALKS IN THE TWILIGHT.
Crown 8vo, 2s. 6d.

NOT QUITE A LADY.
Illustrated. Crown 8vo, 2s. 6d.

ONLY A GIRL-WIFE.
Illustrated. Crown 8vo, 2s. 6d.

LONDON:

THE RELIGIOUS TRACT SOCIETY,

4 BOUVERIE ST. AND 65 ST. PAUL'S CHURCHYARD.

TALES BY HESBA STRETTON.

COBWEBS AND CABLES.
    Illustrated. Imperial 16mo, gilt edges, 5s.

HALF-BROTHERS.
    Illustrated. Crown 8vo, 5s.

CAROLA.
    Illustrated. Crown 8vo, 3s. 6d.

THROUGH A NEEDLE'S EYE.
    Illustrated. Large crown 8vo, full gilt, 3s. 6d.

BEDE'S CHARITY.
    Illustrated. Crown 8vo, gilt edges, 2s. 6d.

IN THE HOLLOW OF HIS HAND. Illustrated. 2s.

CHILDREN OF CLOVERLEY. Illustrated. 2s.

ENOCH RODEN'S TRAINING. Illustrated. 2s.

FERN'S HOLLOW. Illustrated. 2s.

FISHERS OF DERBY HAVEN. Illustrated. 2s.

PILGRIM STREET. Illustrated. 2s.

A THORNY PATH. Illustrated. 2s.

ALONE IN LONDON. Illustrated. 1s. 6d.

CASSY. Illustrated. 1s. 6d.

THE LORD'S PURSE-BEARERS. Illustrated. 1s. 6d.

THE CREW OF THE DOLPHIN. Illustrated. 1s. 6d.

THE KING'S SERVANTS. Illustrated. 1s. 6d.

LITTLE MEG'S CHILDREN. Illustrated. 1s. 6d.

LOST GIP. Illustrated. 1s. 6d.

MAX KRÖMER. Illustrated. 1s. 6d.

THE STORM OF LIFE. Illustrated. 1s. 6d.

LONDON:
THE RELIGIOUS TRACT SOCIETY,
4 BOUVERIE ST. AND 65 ST. PAUL'S CHURCHYARD.

TALES BY MRS. O. F. WALTON.

WAS I RIGHT?
Illustrated. Large crown 8vo, 3s. 6d.

A PEEP BEHIND THE SCENES.
Illustrated. Large crown 8vo, 3s. 6d.
Cheaper Edition, crown 8vo, Illustrated, 2s.

SCENES IN THE LIFE OF AN OLD ARMCHAIR ;
Or, Shadows. Illustrated. Imperial 16mo, cloth, gilt edges, 3s. 6d.

THE WONDERFUL DOOR ;
Or, Nemo. Illustrated. 2s.

OLIVE'S STORY ;
Or, Life at Ravenscliffe. Illustrated. 2s.

WINTER'S FOLLY.
Illustrated. 2s.

MY LITTLE CORNER.
Illustrated. 1s. 6d.

MY MATES AND I.
Illustrated. 1s. 6d.

AUDREY ;
Or, Children of Light. Illustrated. 1s.

CHRISTIE'S OLD ORGAN ;
Or, Home, Sweet Home. Illustrated. 1s.

CHRISTIE, THE KING'S SERVANT.
A Sequel to 'Christie's Old Organ.' Illustrated. 1s.

LITTLE FAITH ;
Or, The Child of the Toy-Stall. Illustrated. 1s.

THE MYSTERIOUS HOUSE.
Illustrated. 1s.

NOBODY LOVES ME.
Illustrations. 1s.

PICTURES AND STORIES FROM QUEEN VIC-
TORIA'S LIFE.
With Forty Illustrations. 1s.

POPPY'S PRESENTS.
Illustrated. 1s.

SAVED AT SEA.
A Lighthouse Story. Illustrated. 1s.

TAKEN OR LEFT.
Illustrated. 1s.

LONDON:
THE RELIGIOUS TRACT SOCIETY,
4 BOUVERIE ST. AND 65 ST. PAUL'S CHURCHYARD.

STORIES BY EGLANTON THORNE.

THE BLESSEDNESS OF IRENE FARQUHAR.
With Frontispiece. Crown 8vo, 2s. 6d.

HER OWN WAY.
Illustrated. Crown 8vo, 2s. 6d.

MY BROTHER'S FRIEND.
With Frontispiece. Crown 8vo, 2s. 6d.

IN LONDON FIELDS.
A Story of a Child's Life. Illustrated. Crown 8vo, 2s.

AS MANY AS TOUCHED HIM.
Illustrated. Crown 8vo, 1s.

THE COTTAGE BY THE LINN.
Illustrated. Crown 8vo, 1s.

THE ELDER BROTHER.
Illustrated. Crown 8vo, 1s.

IT'S ALL REAL TRUE.
The Story of a Child's Difficulties. Illustrated. Crown 8vo, 1s.

A LITTLE PROTESTANT IN ROME.
Illustrated. Crown 8vo, 1s.

THE OLD WORCESTER JUG.
Illustrated. Crown 8vo, 1s.

PHIL'S MOTHER.
Illustrated. Crown 8vo, 1s.

A SHAM PRINCESS.
Illustrated. Crown 8vo, 1s.

LONDON:
THE RELIGIOUS TRACT SOCIETY,
4 BOUVERIE ST. AND 65 ST. PAUL'S CHURCHYARD.